Published by Coffee-Bum Publishing part of the Jacqui Shepherd Children's Author Brand

First edition 2023

ISBN: 9798418215055

**The Delightful Dinos
Run-o-saurus: The running dinosaur**
by Jacqui Shepherd

A book about the joy of running.

Copy editor and Proofreader:
Michele L.Mathews of Beach Girl Publishing LLC

Illustrations and book design: SKlakina

The Delightful Dinos

Run-o-saurus:
The running dinosaur

This book is dedicated to my daughter, Kristen. When she was little she never sat still for long. She is still always on the move. Her endless energy fills my heart with joy.

I love you, Kristen.

Run-o-saurus loves to run.

She rarely walks.
"Why walk when you can run?" she says.

It's not that she is in a hurry.

She just likes running.

Sometimes she jogs slowly, and sometimes she runs at a steady pace.

Sometimes she sprints, running at her very fastest.

She does stretches to warm up her muscles
before she runs,

and then stretches afterward to cool down.

Running is good exercise.

It keeps Run-o-saurus fit and healthy.

Run-o-saurus likes to run with running shoes on,

but she likes to run barefoot just as much.

She runs inside and outside.

She runs wherever she is going…

…and then runs back again.

She even runs in one place.

Run-o-saurus thinks running is the best.

She likes how free it makes her feel.

The more she practices her running, the faster she gets.

She likes speeding past things.

But she's always careful, so she doesn't crash into anything…

…or anyone.

When Mommy Dinosaur needs something
in a hurry,

she asks Run-o-saurus.

Run-o-saurus likes to run races with her friends,

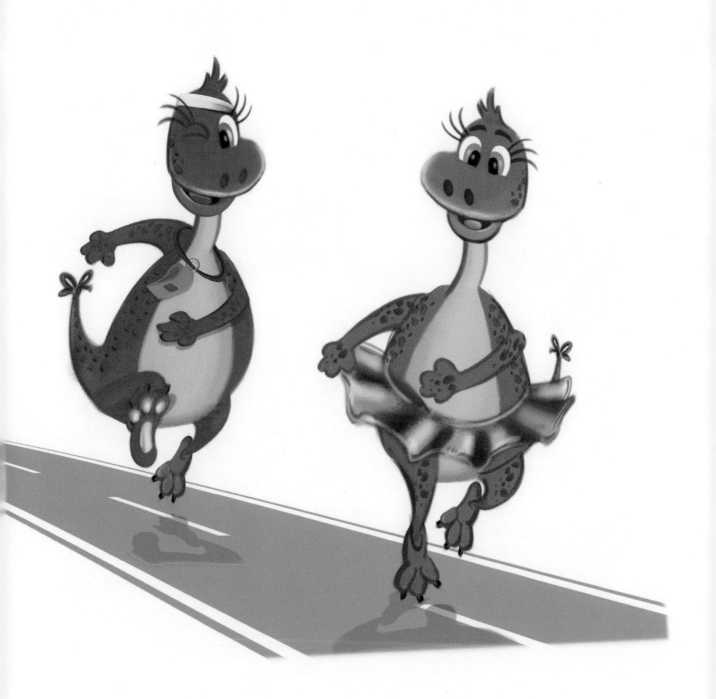

and sometimes she lets them win.

Now and then, Run-o-saurus gets all the dinosaurs to join her for a big fun run.

"Running can be fun for everyone,"
Run-o-saurus says.

Some running safety tips from Run-o-saurus:

* Never run while carrying sharp or breakable objects.
* Never run into the street.
* Always look where you are running.
* Always keep your hands free when you run. If you trip, they'll help you catch yourself.
* Don't run in busy, crowded places.
* Don't run in cluttered, cramped places.
* Don't run on slippery surfaces.
* Remember to stretch to warm up your muscles before you run.
* Remember to stretch to cool down your muscles after you run.

Other books in
The Delightful Dinos series

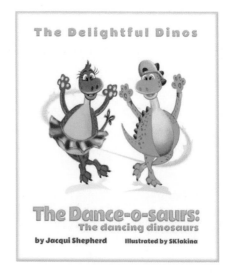

Get them all!

Dear Reader,

Thank you for choosing Run-o-saurus: The running dinosaur.

If you had fun with Run-o-saurus, please take a moment to post a review on Amazon.

Your support makes a BIG difference.

Reviews from awesome readers like you will help others to discover and read this book, too.

Thank you!

About the author

I inherited my talent for storytelling from my father and first began creating my own stories to amuse my children. I strive to entertain, encourage and empower children through my stories.

My goal is to create engaging stories that leave children and parents with happy hearts and smiling faces.

I believe it is important to read to a child and to teach a child to love reading. I currently reside in sunny South Africa.

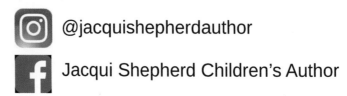

@jacquishepherdauthor

Jacqui Shepherd Children's Author

About the illustrator

When I was a little girl, I "lived" in the fabulous drawings of my grandfather. He was an artist. I dreamed of learning to draw the same colorful, attractive and funny illustrations. I am very glad that my dream came true and I can delight children and their parents with my drawings.

Believe in your dreams! Welcome to my world!

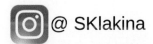 @ SKlakina

Portfolio: www.behance.net/SKlakina
sklakina@gmail.com
Books available on Amazon.com

Other books by Jacqui Shepherd

Animal Adventures series

Eddie gets a fright!
The rabbit and the fox
Jojo's journey
Wally gets a tummy ache!
The proud old owl
The little grey horse who
loved to run
The monkey who wanted
to be different
Pinky breaks the rules
Ruby Right
The unkind buffalo

Bug stories series

Aggi the ant
Bongi the beetle
Cobus the cockroach
Fatima the fly
Gonzo the grasshopper
Lala the ladybug
Mindi the moth
Sam the spider
Solomon the snail
Webster the worm

Sea stories series

Cale the crab
Dabi the dolphin
Elroy the eel
Finny the fish
Ozzy the octopus
Patti the prawn
Safina the shark
Suzy the seal
Tagu the turtle
Wadi the whale

Farm-tastic series

Invisi-bull
Enor-mouse
Hap-pig-ness
G-lamb-orous
Hope-frog-ly
Un-hap-puppy
Imag-hen-ation
Fear-foal
For-goat-ten
Dis-cow-very

Superpower Imagination

Goo on my shoe

To find out more about Jacqui and her world of books, visit her website, and if you want to stay updated about new books, subscribe to her mailing list or follow her on Amazon.

https://jacquishepherd.com/

Use the social media icons on Jacqui's website to follow her on Facebook, Instagram, Twitter, and more.

Printed in Great Britain
by Amazon

20076795R00025